In-Betweeny-Weeny
Written by Sally Hooper

ISBN 978-1-78222-980-3

Book design, layout and production management by Into Print
www.intoprint.net
+44 (0)1604 832149

In a house on a hill
lived a little little
named Ziggy Wiggy.

Ziggy Wiggy's mama thought
Zig was the kindest, most
compassionate and loving
little in all the land...

Ziggy Wiggy wasn't
a baby, and wasn't
a biggy either.

4

$3\frac{1}{2}$

Zig was right
in-betweeny-weeny.

Ziggy Wiggy knew how to eat like a biggy...

Ziggy Wiggy was learning to swim.

Sometimes Zig could paddle all the way across the pool with **giant reaching arms** and **kicking feet.**

Then next time...

...Zig would sink!

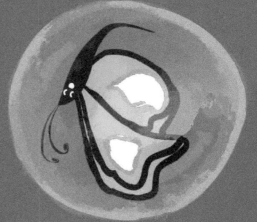

"**That's okay, no big deal,** sometimes that happens when you're still learning and I love you **in-betweeny-weeny.**"

Ziggy Wiggy
could talk like
a biggy.

Zig was so curious and loved to ask questions and use big fancy words.

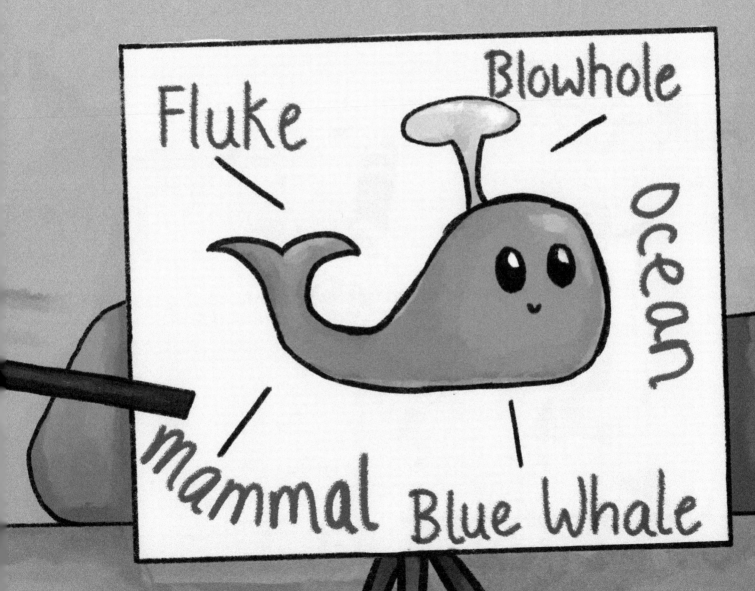

But sometimes Ziggy Wiggy's words seemed to get stuck and were hard to get out...

When this happened,
Ziggy Wiggy remembered
what Mama always said.

"That's okay, no big deal, sometimes that happens when you're still learning and I love you **in-betweeny-weeny.**"

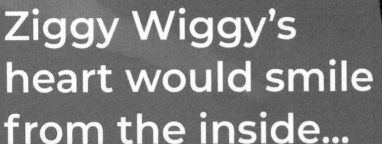

Ziggy Wiggy's heart would smile from the inside...

...Zig would take a deep breath and try again, because Zig was still learning.

At night in that house on the hill,
Ziggy Wiggy's mama cuddled Zig
close and tucked Zig in tight.

She always said...

"I think you're fun to be around clean or messy."

"I'm proud of you if you're swimming or sinking.."

"and whether your words are easy to find or hard to get out..."

"...I love you in-betweeny-weeny, to the stars and back again."

About The Illustrators

Rebecca Wheele is an illustrator and designer as well as one of the directors at World Game-Changers. She leads the LEG (Life Enhancing Goal) 'Awareness-Raising and Mindful Communication' and believes in the importance of using creativity in education to help get important messages across in a fun and inspiring way.

Dina Goldman is a high school student who is passionate about art as a vehicle for storytelling and expressing ideas and feelings. During her Junior year, Dina was accepted into Oxbow Art School where she participated in an intensive semester of studio art-making combined with rigorous academics. She also works at a local art studio teaching children how to draw and paint using many mediums. Dina looks forward to furthering her artistic studies in college.

About The Author

Sally Hooper is a career educator and champion for children. She is an educational & behavioral consultant, working with school districts helping them integrate principles of Applied Behavior Analysis into classrooms. Sally also works privately for families, equipping caregivers with effective, evidence-based strategies, and helping them optimize their skills to get back to enjoying time together.

As Vice-Chair of World Game Changers North America, it's Sally's mission to help grown-ups raise global peace leaders. Why not start young? Afterall, the earlier the easier.

To learn more, visit: www.worldgamechangers.org

Ingram Content Group UK Ltd.
Milton Keynes UK
UKHW051845090323
418299UK00009B/65